John L. Motley

The Causes of the American Civil War

A letter to the London Times

John L. Motley

The Causes of the American Civil War
A letter to the London Times

ISBN/EAN: 9783337220907

Printed in Europe, USA, Canada, Australia, Japan

Cover: Foto ©Andreas Hilbeck / pixelio.de

More available books at **www.hansebooks.com**

THE CAUSES

OF THE

AMERICAN CIVIL WAR.

A LETTER TO THE LONDON TIMES.

BY

JOHN LOTHROP MOTLEY, LL.D., D.C.L.

AUTHOR OF "THE RISE OF THE DUTCH REPUBLIC," AND "HISTORY OF THE UNITED
NETHERLANDS."

NEW YORK:

JAMES G. GREGORY.

(SUCCESSOR TO W. A. TOWNSEND & CO.)

NO. 46 WALKER STREET.

1861.

THE CAUSES

OF THE

AMERICAN CIVIL WAR.

To THE EDITOR OF THE LONDON TIMES:

The *de facto* question in America has been referred at last to the dread arbitrament of civil war. Time and events must determine whether the "great Republic" is to disappear from the roll of nations, or whether it is destined to survive the storm which has gathered over its head. There is, perhaps, a readiness in England to prejudge the case; a disposition not to exult in our downfall, but to accept the fact; for nations, as well as individuals, may often be addressed in the pathetic language of the poet—

> "Donec eris felix. multos numerabis amicos,
> Tempora cum fuerint nubila, nullus erit."

Yet the trial by the ordeal of battle has hardly commenced, and it would be presumptuous to affect to penetrate the veil of even the immediate future. But the question *de jure* is a different one. The right and the wrong belong to the past, are hidden by no veil, and may easily be read by all who are not wilfully blind.

Yet it is often asked, Why have the Americans taken up arms? Why has the United States government plunged into what is sometimes called "this wicked war?" Especially it is thought amazing in England that the President should have recently called for a great army of volunteers and regulars, and that the inhabitants of the free states should have sprung forward as one man at his call, like men suddenly relieved from a spell. It would have been amazing had the call been longer delayed. The national flag, insulted and defied for many months, had at last been lowered, after the most astonishing kind of siege recorded in history, to an armed and organized.rebellion; and a prominent personage in the government of the Southern "Confederacy" is reported to have proclaimed amid the exultations of victory that before the first of May the same cherished emblem of our nationality should be struck from the Capitol at Washington. An advance of the "Confederate troops" upon the city; the flight or captivity of the President and his Cabinet; the seizure of the national archives, the national title deeds, and the whole national machinery of foreign intercourse and internal administration by the Confederates; and the proclamation from the American palladium itself of the Montgomery Constitution in place of the one devised by Washington, Madison, Hamilton, and Jay—a Constitution in which slavery should be the universal law of the land, the corner-stone of the political edifice— were events which seemed for a few days of intense anxiety almost probable.

Had this really been the result without a blow struck in defence of the national government and the old constitution, it is certain that the contumely poured forth upon the free states by their domestic enemies and by the world at large would have been as richly deserved as it would have been amply bestowed. At present such a catastrophe seems to have been averted. But the levy in mass of such a vast number of armed men in the free states, in swift response to the call of the President, shows how deep and pervading is the attachment to the constitution and to the flag of Union in the hearts of the nineteen millions who inhabit those states. It is confidently believed, too, that the sentiment is not wholly extinguished in the nine million white men who dwell in the slave states, and that, on the contrary, there exists a large party throughout that country who believe that the Union furnishes a better protection for life, property, law, civilization, and liberty, than even the indefinite extension of African slavery can do.

At any rate, the loyalty of the free states has proved more intense and passionate than it had ever been supposed to be before. It is recognized throughout their whole people that the constitution of 1787 had made us a *nation*. The efforts of a certain class of politicians for a long period had been to reduce our commonwealth to a confederacy. So long as their efforts had been confined to argument, it was considered sufficient to answer the argument; but now that secession, instead of remaining a topic of vehement and subtle discussion, has expanded into armed and fierce rebellion and revolution, civil war is the inevitable result. It is the result foretold by sagacious statesmen almost a generation ago, in the days of the tariff "nullification." "To begin with nullification," said Daniel Webster in 1833, "with the

avowed intention, nevertheless, not to proceed to secession, dismemberment, and general revolution, is as if
one were to take the plunge of Niagara, and cry out
that he would stop half-way down." And now the
plunge of secession has been taken, and we are all
struggling in the vortex of general revolution.

The body politic known for seventy years as the
United States of America *is not a confederacy, not a
compact of sovereign states, not a copartnership ; it is a
commonwealth*, of which the constitution drawn up at
Philadelphia by the Convention of 1787, over which
Washington presided, is the organic, fundamental law.
We had already had enough of a confederacy. The thirteen rebel provinces, afterwards the thirteen original
independent states of America, had been united to each
other during the revolutionary war by articles of confederacy. "*The said states* hereby enter into a firm
league of friendship *with each other*." Such was the
language of 1781, and the league or treaty thus drawn
up was ratified, not by the *people* of the states, but by
the state governments—the legislative and executive
bodies, namely, in their corporate capacity.

The Continental Congress, which was the central ad-
ministrative board during this epoch, was a diet of
envoys from sovereign states. It had *no power* to act *on
individuals*. It could not *command* the states. It could
move only by requisitions and recommendations. Its
functions were essentially diplomatic, like those of the
States-General of the old Dutch republic, like those of
the modern Germanic confederation.

We were a league of petty sovereignties. When the
war had ceased, when our independence had been ac-

knowledged in 1783, we sank rapidly into a condition of utter impotence, imbecility, anarchy. We had achieved our independence, but we had not constructed a nation. We were not a body politic. No laws could be enforced, no insurrections suppressed, no debt collected. Neither property nor life was secure. Great Britain had made a treaty of peace with us, but she scornfully declined a treaty of commerce and amity; not because we had been rebels, but because we were not a state—because we were a mere dissolving league of jarring provinces, incapable of guarantying the stipulations of any commercial treaty. We were unable even to fulfil the condition of the treaty of peace and enforce the stipulated collection of debts due to British subjects; and Great Britain refused, in consequence, to give up the military posts which she held within our frontiers.

For twelve years after the acknowledgment of our *independence* we were mortified by the spectacle of foreign soldiers occupying a long chain of fortresses south of the great lakes and upon our own soil. We were a confederacy. We were sovereign states. And these were the fruits of such a confederacy and such sovereignty. It was, until the immediate present, the darkest hour of our history. But there were patriotic and sagacious men in those days, and their efforts at last rescued us from the condition of a confederacy. The " Constitution of the United States" was an organic law, enacted by the sovereign people of that whole territory which is commonly called in geographics and histories the United States of America. It was empowered to act directly, by its own legislative, judicial and executive machinery, upon every individual in the country.

It could seize his property, it could take his life, for causes of which itself was the judge. The states were distinctly prohibited from opposing its decrees, or from exercising any of the great functions of sovereignty. The Union alone was supreme, "anything in the constitution and laws of the states to the contrary notwithstanding." Of what significance, then, was the title of "sovereign" states, arrogated in later days by communities which had voluntarily abdicated the most vital attributes of sovereignty?

But, indeed, the words "sovereign" and "sovereignty" are purely inapplicable to the American system. In the Declaration of independence the provinces declare themselves "free and independent states," but the men of those days knew that the word "sovereign" was a term of feudal origin. When their connection with a time-honored feudal monarchy was abruptly severed the word "sovereign" had no meaning for us. A sovereign is one who acknowledges no superior, who possesses the highest authority without control, who is supreme in power. How could any one state of the United States claim such characteristics at all, least of all after its inhabitants, in their primary assemblies, had voted to submit themselves, without limitation of time, to a constitution which was declared supreme? The only intelligible source of power in a country beginning its history *de novo* after a revolution, in a land never subjected to military or feudal conquest, is the will of the people of the whole land as expressed by a majority. At the present moment, unless the southern revolution shall prove successful, the United States government is a fact, an established authority. In the period between

1783 and 1787 we were in chaos. In May of 1787 the convention met at Philadelphia, and, after some months' deliberation, adopted with unprecedented unanimity the project of the great law, which, so soon as it should be accepted by the people, was to be known as the Constitution of the United States.

It was not a compact. Who ever heard of a compact to which there were no parties, or who ever heard of a compact made by a single party with himself? Yet the name of no state is mentioned in the whole document; the states themselves are only mentioned to receive commands or prohibitions, and the "people of the United States" is the single party by whom alone the instrument is executed.

The constitution was not drawn up by the states, it was not promulgated in the name of the states, it was not ratified by the states. The states never acceded to it, and possess no power to secede from it. It "was ordained and established" over the states by a power superior to the states—by the people of the whole land in their aggregate capacity, acting through conventions of delegates expressly chosen for the purpose within each state, independently of the state governments, after the project had been framed.

There had always been two parties in the country during the brief but pregnant period between the abjuration of British authority and the adoption of the Constitution of 1787. There was a party advocating state rights and local self-government in its largest sense, and a party favoring a more consolidated and national government. The National or Federal party triumphed in the adoption of the new government. It was strenuously supported and bitterly opposed on exactly the same grounds. Its friends and foes both agreed that it had put an end to the system of confederacy. Whether it were an advantageous or a noxious change, all agreed that the thing had been done.

" In all our deliberations (says the letter accompanying and recommending the constitution to the people) we kept steadily in view that which appeared to us the greatest interest of every true American, the *consolidation of our Union*, in which is involved our prosperity, safety, perhaps *our national existence*." (*Journal of the Convention*, 1 Story, 368.)

And an eloquent opponent denounced the project for this very same reason :

" That this is a consolidated government (said Henry) is demonstrably clear. The language is, ' we the people,' instead of ' we the states.' It must be one great consolidated national government of the people of all the states."

And the Supreme Court of the United States, after the government had been established, held this language in an important case, " Gibbons agt. Ogden :"

" It has been said that the states were sovereign, were completely independent, and were connected with each other by a league. This is true. But when these allied sovereignties converted their league into a government, when they converted their Congress of ambassadors into a legislature, empowered to enact laws, the whole character in which the states appear underwent a change."

There was never a disposition in any quarter in the early days of our constitutional history to deny this great fundamental principle of the Republic.

"In the most elaborate expositions of the constitution by its friends (says Justice Story), its character *as a permanent form* of government, as a fundamental law, as a supreme rule, which no state was at liberty to disregard, to suspend, or to annul, was constantly admitted and insisted upon." (1 Story, 325.)

The fears of its opponents, then, were that the new system would lead to a strong, to an over-centralized government. The fears of its friends were that the central power of theory would prove inefficient to cope with the local, or state forces, in practice. The inexperience of the last thirty years and the catastrophe of the present year, have shown which class of fears were the more reasonable.

Had the Union thus established in 1787 been a confederacy, it might have been argued, with more or less plausibility, that the states which peaceably acceded to it, might at pleasure peaceably secede from it. It is none the less true that such a proceeding would have stamped the members of the convention—Washington, Madison, Jay, Hamilton and their colleagues — with utter incompetence; for nothing can be historically more certain than that their object was to extricate us from the anarchy to which that principle had brought us.

" *However gross a heresy it may be* (say the federalists, recommending the new constitution), to maintain that a party to a compact has a right to revoke that compact, the doctrine has had respectable advocates. The *possibility* of such a question shows the necessity of laying the foundation of our national government deeper than in the mere sanction of delegated author-

ity.   The fabric of American empire ought to rest on
the solid basis of the consent of the people."

Certainly, the most venerated expounders of the constitution—Jay, Marshall, Hamilton, Kent, Story, Webster—were of opinion that the intention of the convention to establish a permanent consolidated government,
a single commonwealth, had been completely successful.

"The great and fundamental defect of the confederation of 1781 (says Chancellor Kent), which led to its
eventual overthrow, was that, in imitation of all former
confederacies, it carried the decrees of the federal council
to the states in their sovereign capacity.   The great and
incurable defect of all former federal governments, such
as the Amphictyonic, Achæan, and Lycian Confederacies,
and the Germanic, Helvetic, Hanseatic and Dutch Republics, is that they were *sovereignties over sovereignties*.
The first effort to relieve the people of the country from
this state of national degradation and ruin came from
Virginia.   The general convention afterwards met at
Philadelphia in May, 1787.   The plan was submitted to
a convention of delegates chosen by the people at large
in each state for assent and ratification.   Such a mea-
sure was laying the foundations of the fabric of our
national polity where alone they ought to be laid—on the
broad consent of the people."   (1 Kent, 225.)

It is true that the consent of the people was given by
the inhabitants voting in each state ; but in what other
conceivable way could the people of the whole country
have voted ?   "They assembled in the several states,"
said Story ; " but where else could they assemble?"

*Secession is, in brief, the return to chaos from which
we emerged three-quarters of a century since.*   No logi-

cal sequence can be more perfect. If one state has a right to secede to-day, asserting what it calls its sovereignty, another may, and probably will, do the same to-morrow, a third on the next day, and so on, until there are none to secede from. Granted the premises that each state may peaceably secede from the Union, it follows that a county may peaceably secede from a state, and a town from a county, until there is nothing left but a horde of individuals all seceding from each other. The theory that the people of a whole country in their aggregate capacity are supreme is intelligible; and it has been a fact, also, in America for seventy years. But it is impossible to show, if the people of a state be sovereign, that the people of a county or of a village, and the individuals of the village, are not equally sovereign, and justified in "resuming their sovereignty" when their interest or their caprice seems to impel them. The process of disintegration brings back the community to barbarism, precisely as its converse has built up commonwealths—whether empires, kingdoms, or republics—out of original barbarism.

Established authority, whatever the theory of its origin, is a fact. It should never be lightly or capriciously overturned. They who venture on the attempt should weigh well the responsibility which is upon them. Above all, they must expect to be arraigned for their deeds before the tribunal of the civilized world and of future ages—a court of last appeal, the code of which is based on the Divine principles of right and reason, which are dispassionate and eternal. No man, on either side of the Atlantic, with Anglo-Saxon blood in his veins, will dispute the right of a people, or of any portion of a people, to rise against oppression, to demand redress of grievances, and in case of denial of justice to take up arms to vindicate the sacred principles of liberty. Few Englishmen or Americans will deny that the source of government is the consent of the governed, or that any nation has the right to govern itself according to its own will. When the silent consent is changed to fierce remonstrance the revolution is impending.

The right of revolution is indisputable. It is written on the whole record of our race. British and American history is made up of rebellion and revolution. Many of the crowned kings were rebels or usurpers. Hampden, Pym and Oliver Cromwell; Washington, Adams and Jefferson—all were rebels. It is no word of reproach. But these men all knew the work they had set themselves to do. They never called their rebellion "peaceable secession." They were sustained by the consciousness of right when they overthrew established authority, but they meant to overthrow it. They meant rebellion, civil war, bloodshed, infinite suffering for themselves and their whole generation, for they accounted them welcome substitutes for insulted liberty and violated right. There can be nothing plainer, then, than the American right of revolution. But, then, it should be called revolution. "Secession, as a revolutionary right," said Daniel Webster in the Senate, nearly thirty years ago, in words that now sound prophetic— "is intelligible. As a right to be proclaimed in *the midst of civil commotions, and asserted at the head of armies,* I can understand it. But as a practical right, existing under the constitution, and in conformity with its provisions, it seems to be nothing but an absurdity, for it supposes resistance to government under the authority of government itself; it supposes dismemberment without violating the principles of Union; it supposes the violation of oaths without responsibility; it supposes opposition to law without crime; it supposes the total overthrow of government without revolution."

The men who had conducted the American people through a long and fearful revolution were the founders of the new commonwealth which permanently superseded the subverted authority of the crown. They placed the foundations on the unbiassed, untrammelled consent of the people. They were sick of leagues, of petty sovereignties, of governments which could not govern a single individual. The framers of the constitution, which has now endured three-quarters of a century, and under which the nation has made a material and intellectual progress never surpassed in history, were not such triflers as to be ignorant of the consequences of their own acts. The constitution which they offered, and which the people adopted as its own, talked not of sovereign states—spoke not the word confederacy. In the very preamble to the instrument are inserted the vital words which show its character, "We, *the people* of the United States, to insure a more perfect union, and to secure the blessings of liberty for ourselves and our posterity, *do ordain and establish this constitution*." *Sic volo, sic jubeo.* It is the language of a sovereign solemnly speaking to the world. It is the promulgation of a great law, the *norma agendi* of a new commonwealth. It is no compact.

" A compact (says Blackstone) is a promise proceeding from us. Law is a command directed to us. The language of a compact is, We will or will not do this; that of a law is, Thou shalt or shalt not do it." (1 B. 38, 44, 45.)

And this is throughout the language of the constitution. Congress shall do this; the President shall do that; the states shall not exercise this or that power. Witness, for example, the important clauses by which the " sovereign" states are shorn of all the great attributes of sovereignty—no state shall coin money, nor emit bills of credit, nor pass *ex post facto* laws, nor laws impairing the obligation of contracts, nor maintain armies and navies, nor grant letters of marque, nor make compacts with other states, nor hold intercourse with foreign powers, nor grant titles of nobility; and that most significant phrase, " this constitution, and the laws made in pursuance thereof, *shall be the supreme law of the land.*"

Could language be more imperial? Could the claim to state " sovereignty" be more completely disposed of at a word? How can that be sovereign, acknowledging no superior, supreme, which has voluntarily accepted a supreme law from something which it acknowledges as superior?

The constitution is perpetual, not provisional or temporary. It is made for all time—" for ourselves and our posterity." It is absolute within its sphere. " This constitution shall be the supreme law of the land, anything in the constitution or laws of a state to the contrary notwithstanding." Of what value, then, is a law of a state declaring its connection with the Union dissolved? The constitution remains supreme, and is bound to assert its supremacy till overpowered by force. The use of force

—of armies and navies of whatever strength—in order to compel obedience to the civil and constitutional authority, *is not "wicked war," is not civil war, is not war at all.* So long as it exists the government is obliged to put forth its strength when assailed. The President, who has taken an oath before God and man to maintain the constitution and laws, is perjured if he yields the constitution and laws to armed rebellion without a struggle. He knows nothing of states. Within the sphere of the United States government he deals with individuals only, citizens of the great republic, in whatever portion of it they may happen to live. He has no choice but to enforce the laws of the republic wherever they may be resisted. When he is overpowered, the government ceases to exist. The Union is gone, and Massachusetts, Rhode Island, and Ohio are as much separated from each other as they are from Georgia or Louisiana. Anarchy has returned upon us. The dismemberment of the commonwealth is complete. We are again in the chaos of 1785.

But it is sometimes asked why the constitution did not make a special provision against the right of secession. How could it do so? The people created a constitution over the whole land, with certain defined, accurately enumerated powers, and among these were all the chief attributes of sovereignty. It was forbidden to a state to coin money, to keep armies and navies, to make compacts with other states, to hold intercourse with foreign nations, to oppose the authority of the government. To do any one of these things is to secede, for it would be physically impossible to do any one of them without secession. It would have been puerile for the constitution

2

to say formally to each state, "Thou shalt not secede."
The constitution, being the supreme law, being perpetual, and having expressly forbidden to the states those
acts without which secession is an impossibility, *would
have been wanting in dignity had it used such super-
fluous phraseology.* This constitution is supreme, whatever laws a state may enact, says the organic law. Was
it necessary to add, "and no state shall enact a law of
secession." To add to a great statute, in which the sovereign authority of the land declares its will, a phrase
such as "and be it further enacted that the said law
shall not be violated," would scarcely seem to strengthen
the statute.

It was accordingly enacted that new states might be
admitted; but no permission was given for a state to
secede.

Provisions were made for the amendment of the constitution from time to time, and it was intended that
those provisions should be stringent. A two-thirds vote
in both Houses of Congress, and a ratification in three
quarters of the whole number of states, are conditions
only to be complied with in grave emergencies. But
the constitution made no provision for its own dissolu-
tion; and if it had done so, it would have been a proceeding quite without example in history. A constitution can only be subverted by revolution, or by foreign
conquest of the land. The revolution may be the result of a successful rebellion. A peaceful revolution
is also conceivable in the case of the United States.
The same power which established the constitution may
justly destroy it. The people of the whole land may
meet, by delegates, in a great national convention, as

they did in 1787, and declare that the constitution no longer answers the purpose for which it was ordained; that it no longer can secure the blessings of liberty for the people in present and future generations, and that it is therefore forever abolished. When that project has been submitted again to the people voting in their primary assemblies, not influenced by fraud or force, the revolution is lawfully accomplished, and the Union is no more.

Such a proceeding is conceivable, although attended with innumerable difficulties and dangers. But these are not so great as those of the civil war into which the action of the seceding states has plunged the country. The division of the national domain and other property, the navigation and police of the great rivers, the arrangement and fortification of frontiers, the transit of the isthmus, the mouth of the Mississippi, the control of the Gulf of Mexico, these are significant phrases which have an appalling sound; for there is not one of them that does not contain the seeds of war. In any separation, however accomplished, these difficulties must be dealt with, but there would seem less hope of arriving at a peaceful settlement of them now that the action of the seceding states has been so precipitate and lawless. For a single state, one after another, to resume those functions of sovereignty which it had unconditionally abdicated when its people ratified the constitution of 1787; to seize forts, arsenals, custom-houses, post-offices, mints, and other valuable property of the Union, paid for by the treasure of the Union, was not the exercise of a legal function, but it was rebellion, treason, and plunder.

It is strange that Englishmen should find difficulty in understanding that the United States government is a nation among the nations of the earth; a constituted authority, which may be overthrown by violence, as may be the fate of any state, whether kingdom or republic, but which is false to the people if it does not its best to preserve them from the horrors of anarchy, even at the cost of blood. The "United States" happens to be a plural title, but the commonwealth thus designated is a unit, "*e pluribus unum.*" *The Union alone is clothed with imperial attributes; the Union alone is known and recognized in the family of nations; the Union alone holds the purse and the sword*, regulates foreign intercourse, imposes taxes on foreign commerce, makes war and concludes peace. The armies, the navies, the militia, belong to the Union alone; and the president is commander-in-chief of all. No state can keep troops or fleets. What man in the civilized world has not heard of the United States; what man in England can tell the names of all the individual states? And yet, with hardly a superficial examination of our history and our constitution, men talk glibly about a confederacy, a compact, a copartnership, and the right of a state to secede at pleasure, not knowing that by admitting such loose phraseology and such imaginary rights, we should violate the first principles of our political organization, should fly in the face of our history, should trample under foot the teachings of Jay, Hamilton, Washington, Marshall, Madison, Dane, Kent, Story, and Webster, and accepting only the dogmas of Mr. Calhoun as infallible, surrender forever our national laws and our national existence.

Englishmen themselves live in a united empire; but if the kingdom of Scotland should secede, should seize all the national property, forts, arsenals, and public treasure on its soil, organize an army, send forth foreign ministers to Louis Napoleon, the Emperor of Austria, and other powers, issue invitations to all the pirates of the world to prey upon English commerce, screening their piracy from punishment by the banner of Scotland, and should announce its intention of planting that flag upon Buckingham Palace, it is probable that a blow or two would be struck to defend the national honor and the national existence, without fear that the civil war would be denounced as wicked and fratricidal. Yet it would be difficult to show that the state of Florida, for example, a Spanish province, purchased for national purposes some forty years ago by the United States government for several millions, and fortified and furnished with navy yards for national uses at a national expense of many more millions, and numbering at this moment a population of only eighty thousand white men, should be more entitled to resume its original sovereignty than the ancient kingdom of William the Lion and Robert Bruce.

The terms of the treaty between England and Scotland were perpetual, and so is the Constitution of the United States. The United Empire may be destroyed by revolution and war, and so may the United States; but a peaceful and legal dismemberment without the consent of the majority of the whole people is an impossibility.

But it is sometimes said that the American Republic originated in secession from the mother country, and that it is unreasonable of the Union to resist the seceding movement on the part of the new Confederacy. But it so happens that the one case suggests the other only by the association of contrast. The thirteen colonies did not intend to secede from the British empire. They were forced into secession by a course of policy on the part of the mother country such as no English administration of the present day can be imagined capable of adopting. Those Englishmen in America were loyal to the Crown ; but they exercised the right which cisatlantic or transatlantic Englishmen have always exercised, of resistance to arbitrary government. Taxed without being represented, and insulted by measures taken to enforce the odious but not exorbitant imposts, they did not secede, nor declare their independence. On the contrary, they made every effort to avert such a conclusion. In the words of the " forest-born Demosthenes"—as Lord Byron called the great Virginian, Patrick Henry—the Americans " petitioned, remonstrated, cast themselves at the foot of the throne, and implored its interposition to arrest the tyrannical hands of the ministers and Parliament. But their petition were slighted, their remonstrances procured only additional violence and insult, as they were spurned with contempt from the foot of the throne."

The " Boston massacre," the Boston port-bill, the Boston " tea-party," the battle of Lexington, the battle of Bunker's Hill, were events which long preceded the famous Declaration of Independence. It was not until the colonists felt that redress for grievances was impossible that they took the irrevocable step, and renounced their allegiance to the Crown. The revolution had come at last, they had been forced into it, but they knew that it was revolution, and that they were acting at the peril of their lives. " We must be unanimous in this business," said Hancock; " we must all hang together." " Yes," replied Franklin, " or else we shall all hang separately."

The risk incurred by the colonists was enormous, but the injury to the mother country was comparatively slight. They went out into darkness and danger themselves, but the British empire was not thrown into anarchy and chaos by their secession.

Thus their course was the reverse of that adopted by the South. The prompt secession of seven states because of the constitutional election of a President over the candidates voted for by their people was the redress in advance of grievances which they may, reasonably or unreasonably, have expected, but which had not yet occurred. There is the high authority of the Vice-President of the southern "Confederacy," who declared a week after the election of Mr. Lincoln that the election was not a cause for secession, and that there was no certainty that he would have either the power or the inclination to invade the constitutional rights of the South. In the free states it was held that the resolutions of the convention by which Mr. Lincoln was nominated were scrupulously and conscientiously framed to protect all those constitutional rights. The question of slavery in the territories, of the future extension of slavery, was one which had always been an open question, and on which issue was now joined. But it was no question at all that slavery within a state was sacred from all interference by the general government, or by the free states, or by individuals in those states; and the Chicago Convention strenuously asserted that doctrine.

The question of free trade, which is thrust before the English public by many journals, had no immediate connection with the secession, although doubtless the desire of direct trade with Europe has long been a prominent motive at the South. The Gulf states seceded under the moderate tariff of 1857, for which South Carolina voted side by side with Massachusetts. The latter state, although for political, not economical reasons it thought itself obliged since the secession to sustain the Pennsylvania interest by voting for the absurd Morrill bill, is not in favor of protection. On the contrary, the great manufactories on the Merrimac river have long been independent of protection, and export many million dollars' worth of cotton and other fabrics to foreign countries, underselling or competing with all the world in open market. It would be impossible for any European nation to drive the American manufacturer from the markets of the American continent in the principal articles of cheap clothing for the masses, tariff or no tariff. This is a statistical fact which cannot be impugned.

The secession of the colonies, after years of oppression and grievances for which redress had been sought in vain, left the British empire, 3,000 miles off, in security, with constitution and laws unimpaired, even if its colonial territory were seriously diminished. The secession of the southern states, in contempt of any other remedy for expected grievances, is followed by the destruction of the whole body politic of which they were vital parts.

Not only is the united republic destroyed if the revolution prove successful, but, even if the people of the free states have the enthusiasm and sagacity to reconstruct their Union, and by a new national convention to re-ordain and re-establish the time-honored constitution, still an immense territory is lost. But the extent of that territory is not the principal element in the disaster. The world is wide enough for all. It is the loss of the southern marine frontier which is fatal to the Republic. Florida and the vast Louisiana territory purchased by the Union from foreign countries, and garnished with fortresses at the expense of the Union, are fallen with all these improvements into the hands of a foreign and unfriendly power.

Should the dire misfortune of a war with a great maritime nation, with England or France, for example, befall the Union, its territory, hitherto almost impregnable, might now be open to fleets and armies acting in alliance with a hostile "Confederacy," which has become possessed of an important part of the Union's maritime line of defence. Moreover the Union has twelve thousand ships, numbering more than five million tons, the far greater part of which belongs to the free states, and the vast commerce of the Mississippi and the Gulf of Mexico requires and must receive protection at every hazard.

Is it strange that the Union should make a vigorous, just, and lawful effort to save itself from the chaos from which the constitution of 1787 rescued the country? Who that has read and pondered the history of that dark period does not shudder at the prospect of its return?

But yesterday we were a state—the great republic—prosperous and powerful, with a flag known and honored all over the world. Seventy years ago we were a helpless league of bankrupt and lawless petty sovereignties. We had a currency so degraded that a leg of mutton was cheap at one thousand dollars. The national debt, incurred in the war of independence, had hardly a nominal value, and was considered worthless. The absence of law, order, and security for life and property was as absolute as could be well conceived in a civilized land. Debts could not be collected, courts could enforce no decrees, insurrections could not be suppressed. The army of the confederacy numbered eighty men. From this condition the constitution rescued us.

That great law, reported by the General Convention of 1787, was ratified by the people of all the land voting in each state for a ratifying convention chosen expressly for that purpose. It was promulgated in the name of the people: " We, the people of the United States, in order to form a more perfect Union, and to secure the blessings of liberty for ourselves and our posterity, do ordain and establish this constitution." It was ratified by the people—*not by the states* acting through their governments, legislative and executive, but by the people electing special delegates within each state; and it is important to remember that in none of these ratifying conventions was any reserve made of a state's right to repeal the Union or to secede.

Many criticisms were offered in the various ratifying ordinances, many amendments suggested, but the acceptance of the constitution, the submission to the perpetual law, was in all cases absolute. The language of Virginia was most explicit on this point. "The powers granted under the constitution, *being derived from the people of the United States*, may be *resumed by them* whenever the same shall be perverted to their injury or oppression." That the people of the United States, expressing their will solemnly in national convention, are competent to undo the work of their ancestors, and are fully justified in so doing when the constitution shall be perverted to their injury and oppression, there is no man in the land that doubts. This course has been already indicated as the only peaceful revolution possible; but such a proceeding is very different from the secession ordinance of a single state resuming its sovereignty of its own free will, and without consultation with the rest of the inhabitants of the country.

"There was no reservation (says Justice Story) of any right on the part of any state to dissolve its connection, or to abrogate its dissent, or to suspend the operation of the constitution as to itself."

And thus, when the ratifications had been made, a new commonwealth took its place among the nations of the earth. The effects of the new constitution were almost magical. Order sprang out of chaos. Law resumed its reign; debts were collected; life and property became secure; the national debt was funded and ultimately paid, principal and interest, to the uttermost farthing; the articles of the treaty of peace in 1783 were fulfilled, and Great Britain, having an organized and united state to deal with, entered into a treaty of commerce and amity with us—the first and the best ever negotiated between the two nations. Not the least noble of its articles (the 21st) provided that the acceptance by the citizens or subjects of either country of foreign letters of marque should be treated and *punished as piracy.* Unfortunately, that article and several others were limited to twelve years, and were not subsequently renewed. The debts due to British subjects were collected, and the British government at last surrendered the forts on our soil.

At last we were a nation, with a flag respected abroad and almost idolized at home as the symbol of union and coming greatness, and we entered upon a career of prosperity and progress never surpassed in history. The autonomy of each state, according to which its domestic and interior affairs are subject to the domestic legislature and executive, was secured by the reservation to each state of powers not expressly granted to the Union by the constitution. Supreme within its own orbit, which is traced from the same centre of popular power whence the wider circumference of the general government is described, the individual state is surrounded on all sides by that all-embracing circle. The reserved and unnamed powers are many and important, but the state is closely circumscribed. Thus, a state is forbidden to alter its form of government. "Thou shalt forever remain a republic," says the United States constitution to each individual state. A state is forbidden, above all, to pass any law conflicting with the United States constitution or laws. Moreover, every member of Congress, every member of a state legislature, every executive or judicial officer in the service of the Union or of a separate state, is bound by solemn oath to maintain the United States constitution. This alone would seem to settle the question of secession ordinances. So long as the constitution endures, such an ordinance is merely the act of conspiring and combining individuals, with whom the general government may deal. When it falls in the struggle, and becomes powerless to cope with them, the constitution has been destroyed by violence. *Peaceful acquiescence in such combinations is perjury and treason on the part of the chief magistrate of the country, for which he may be impeached and executed. Yet men speak of Mr. Lincoln as having plunged into wicked war.* They censure him for not negotiating with envoys who came, not to settle grievances, but to demand recognition of the dismemberment of the republic which he had just sworn to maintain.

It is true that the ordinary daily and petty affairs of men come more immediately than larger matters under the cognizance of the state governments, tending thus to foster local patriotism and local allegiance. At the same time, as all controversies between citizens of different states come within the sphere of the federal courts, and as the manifold and conflicting currents of so rapid a national life as the American can rarely be confined within narrow geographical boundaries, it follows that the federal courts, even for domestic purposes as well as foreign, are parts of the daily, visible functions of the body politic. The Union is omnipresent. The custom-house, the court-house, the arsenal, the village post-office, the muskets of the militia, make the authority of the general government a constant fact. Moreover, the restless, migratory character of the population, which rarely permits all the members of one family to remain denizens of any one state, has interlaced the states with each other, and all with the Union to such an extent that a painless excision of a portion of the whole nation is an impossibility. To cut away the pound of flesh and draw no drop of blood surpasses human ingenuity.

Neither the opponents nor friends of the new government in the first generation after its establishment held the doctrine of secession. The states' right party and the federal party disliked or cherished the government because of the general conviction that it was a constituted and centralized authority, permanent and indivisible, like that of any other organized nation. Each party continued to favor or to oppose a strict construction of the instrument; but the doctrine of nullification and secession was a plant of later growth. It was an accepted fact that the United States was not a confederacy. That word was never used in the constitution except once by way of prohibition. We were a nation, not a copartnership, except indeed in the larger sense in which every nation may be considered a copartnership—a copartnership of the present with the past and with the future. To borrow the lofty language of Burke:

"A state ought not to be considered as nothing better than a partnership agreement in a trade of pepper and coffee, calico or tobacco, or some other such low concern, to be taken up for a little temporary interest, and to be dissolved by the fancy of the parties. It is to be looked upon with other reverence, because it is not a partnership in things subservient only to gross animal existence, of a temporary and perishable nature. It is a partnership in all science, a partnership in all art, a partnership in every virtue and in all perfection, a partnership not only between those who are living, but between those who are living, those who are dead, and those who are to be born."

And the simple phrase of the preamble to our constitution is almost as pregnant—"To secure the blessings of liberty to us and our posterity."

But as the innumerable woes of disunion out of which we had been rescued by the constitution began to fade into the past, the allegiance to the Union, in certain regions of the country, seemed rapidly to diminish. *It was reserved to the subtle genius of Mr. Calhoun*, one of the most logical, brilliant and persuasive orators that ever lived, to embody once more in a set of sounding sophisms the main arguments which had been unsuccessfully used in a former generation to prevent the adoption of the constitution, and to exhibit them now as legitimate deductions from the constitution. The memorable tariff controversy was the occasion in which the argument of state sovereignty was put forth in all its strength. In regard to the dispute itself there can be no doubt that the South was in the right, and the North in the wrong. The production by an exaggerated tariff of a revenue so much over and above the wants of government, that it was at last divided among the separate states, and foolishly squandered, was the most triumphant *reductio ad absurdum* that the South could have desired. But it is none the less true that the nullification by a state legislature of a federal law was a greater injury to the whole nation than a foolish tariff, long since repealed, had inflicted. It was a stab to the Union in its vital part. The blow was partially parried, but it may be doubted whether the wound has ever healed.

Tariffs, the protective system, free trade—although

the merits of these questions must be considered as set-
tled by sound thinkers in all civilized lands, must, nevertheless, remain in some countries the subjects of honest
argument and legitimate controversy. When all parts
of a country are represented—and especially in the case
of the United States, where the southern portion has
three-fifths of a certain kind of "property" represented,
while the North has no property represented—reason
should contend with error for victory, trusting to its in-
nate strength. And until after the secession of the Gulf
states the moderate tariff of 1857 was in operation, with
no probability of its repeal. Moreover, the advocates of
the enlightened system of free trade should reflect that
should the fourteen slave states become permanently
united in a separate confederacy, the state of their internal affairs will soon show a remarkable revolution.
*The absence of the Fugitive law will necessarily drive
all the slaves from what are called the border states;* and
he must be a shallow politician who dreams here in
England that free trade with all the world, and direct
taxation for revenue, will be the policy of the new and
expensive military empire which will arise. *Manufac-
tures of cotton and woollen will spring up on every river
and mountain stream in the northern slave states*, the
vast mineral wealth of their territories will require de-
velopment, and the cry for protection to native industry
in one quarter will be as surely heeded as will be that
other cry from the Gulf of Mexico, now partially suppressed for obvious reasons, for the African slave trade.
To establish a great Gulf empire, including Mexico, Central America, Cuba, and other islands, with unlimited
cotton fields and unlimited negroes, this is the golden

vision, in pursuit of which the great republic has been sacrificed, the beneficent constitution subverted. And already the vision has fled, but the work of destruction remains.

The mischief caused by a tariff, however selfish or however absurd, may be temporary. In the last nineteen years there have been four separate tariffs passed by the American Congress, and nothing is more probable than that the suicidal Morrill tariff will receive essential modifications even in the special session of July; but the woes caused by secession and civil war are infinite; and whatever be the result of the contest, this generation is not likely to forget the injuries already inflicted.

The great secession, therefore, of 1860–61 is a rebellion, like any other insurrection against established authority, and has been followed by civil war as its immediate and inevitable consequence. If successful, it is a revolution; and whether successful or not, it will be judged before the tribunal of mankind and posterity according to the eternal laws of reason and justice.

Time and history will decide whether it was a good and sagacious deed to destroy a fabric of so long duration because of the election of Mr. Lincoln; *whether it were wise and noble to substitute over a large portion of the American soil a confederacy of which slavery, in the words of its Vice-President, is the corner-stone, for the old republic, of which Washington with his own hand laid the corner-stone.*

It is conceded by the North that it has received from the Union innumerable blessings. But it would seem that the Union had also conferred benefits on the South. It has carried its mails at a large expense. It has recaptured its fugitive slaves. It has purchased vast tracts of foreign territory, out of which a whole tier of slave states has been constructed. It has annexed Texas. It has made war with Mexico. It has made an offer— not likely to be repeated, however—to purchase Cuba, with its multitude of slaves, at a price, according to report, as large as the sum paid by England for the emancipation of her slaves. Individuals in the free states have expressed themselves freely on slavery, as upon every topic of human thought, and this must ever be the case where there is freedom of the press and of speech. The number of professed abolitionists has hitherto been very small, while the great body of the two principal political parties in the free states have been strongly opposed to them. The Republican party was determined to set bounds to the extension of slavery, while the Democratic party favored that system; but neither had designs secret or avowed against slavery within the states. They knew that the question could only be legally and rationally dealt with by the states themselves. But both the parties, as present events are so signally demonstrating, were imbued with a passionate attachment to the constitution, to the established authority of government, by which alone our laws and our liberty are secured. All parties in the free states are now united as one man, inspired by a noble and generous emotion to vindicate the sullied honor of their flag, and to save their country from the abyss of perdition into which it seemed descending.

Of the ultimate result we have no intention of speaking. Only the presumptuous will venture to lift the veil and affect to read with accuracy coming events, the most momentous perhaps of our times. One result is, however, secured. The Montgomery constitution, with slavery for its corner-stone, is not likely to be accepted, as but lately seemed possible, not only by all the slave states, but even by the border free states; nor to be proclaimed from Washington as the new national law in the name of the United States. *Compromises will no longer be offered by peace conventions, in which slavery is to be made national*, negroes declared property over all the land, and slavery extended over all territories now possessed or hereafter to be acquired. Nor is the United States government yet driven from Washington.

Events are rapidly unrolling themselves, and it will be proved, in course of time, whether the North will remain united in its inflexible purpose, whether the South is as firmly united, or whether a counter revolution will be effected in either section, which must necessarily give the victory to its opponents. We know nothing of the schemes or plans of either government.

The original design of the Republican party was to put an end to the perpetual policy of slavery extension, and acquisition of foreign territory for that purpose, and at the same time to maintain the constitution and the integrity of the republic. This at the South seemed an outrage which justified civil war; for events have amply proved what sagacious statesmen prophesied thirty years ago—that secession is civil war.

If all is to end in negotiation and separation, notwithstanding the almost interminable disputes concerning frontiers, the strongholds in the Gulf and the unshackled navigation of the great rivers throughout their whole length, which, it is probable, will never be abandoned by the North, except as the result of total defeat in the field, it is at any rate certain that *both parties will negotiate more equitably with arms in their hands* than if the unarmed of either section were to deal with the armed. If it comes to permanent separation, too, it is certain that in the commonwealth which will still glory in the name of the United States, and whose people will, doubtless, reëstablish the old constitution with some important amendments, *the word secession will be a sound of woe not to be lightly uttered.* It will have been proved to designate, not a peaceful and natural function of political life, but to be only another expression for revolution, bloodshed, and all the horrors of civil war.

It is probable that a long course of years will be run, and many inconveniences and grievances endured, before any one of the free states secedes from the reconstructed Union.

THE PUBLICATIONS

OF

W. A. Townsend & Company,

No. 46 Walker Street, New York.

The Works of
James Fenimore Cooper.

PEOPLE'S EDITION.—Complete in thirty-four volumes, 12m:
Embracing :

Precaution.	The Bravo.	Afloat and Ashore.
The Spy.	The Heidenmauer.	Miles Wallingford.
The Pioneers.	The Headsman.	The Chainbearer
The Pilot.	The Monikins.	Satanstoe.
Lionel Lincoln.	Homeward Bound.	The Red Skins.
Last of the Mohicans.	Home as Found.	The Crater.
Red Rover.	The Pathfinder.	Jack Tier.
The Prairie.	Me.cedes of Castile.	The Sea Lions.
Travelling Bachelor.	The Deerslayer.	Oak Openings.
Wept of Wish-ton-Wish.	The Two Admirals.	The Ways of the Hour
The Water Witch.	Wing and Wing.	Ned Meyers.
	Wyandotte.	

STYLES AND PRICES.

Embossed muslin, per vol. (each work furnished separately), . . .	$ 1 00
Embossed muslin, the complete set, 34 vols., ...	34 00
Sheep, library style, marble edges, sup. finish, ...	40 00
Half calf or half turkey, plain, ...	55 00
Half calf, extra, full gilt backs, or half calf antique, ...	60 00
Superb calf, or turkey, extra, gilt edges, ...	75 00

DARLEY'S ILLUSTRATED EDITION, with Engravings of Steel and Wood, from Drawings by F. O. C. DARLEY Complete in Thirty-Two Volumes.

The issue of this elegant edition of Cooper's Novels was commenced February 1st, 1859, to be completed in thirty-two months from that date, September 1st, 1861; a volume, containing a novel complete, being issued on the first of each month. The volumes are uniform in size and binding, on superior calendered tinted paper, and each contains TWO ENGRAVINGS ON STEEL, and TWELVE SKETCHES ON WOOD, engraved in a manner altogether superior to ordinary book illustrations. In the series will be included a Biographical Sketch by Wm. Cullen Bryant; a new superb Portrait of MR. COOPER, engraved from an original painting by ELLIOTT, in a style which has never been excelled in America; and a new view of Otsego Hall, Mr. Cooper's late residence.

ORDER OF THE ISSUE OF THE VOLUMES.

The Pioneers.	The Sea Lions.	Oak Openings.
The Red Rover.	The Water-Witch.	The Two Admirals.
Last of the Mohicans.	Homeward Bound.	Deerslayer.
The Spy.	The Monikins.	Mercedes of Castile.
Wyandotte.	Satanstoe.	The Crater.
The Bravo.	Home as Found.	Heidenmauer.
The Pilot.	The Pathfinder.	Afloat and Ashore.
Wept of Wish-ton-Wish.	The Chainbearer.	Miles Wallingford.
The Headsman.	Wing-and-Wing.	Ways of the Hour.
The Prairie.	Jack Tier.	Precaution.
Lionel Lincoln.	The Red Skins.	

Crown octavo, cloth, bevelled edges, gilt back and side, per volume, . $1 50

THE TRAVELLER'S EDITION.

We are now issuing an edition of Cooper's Novels, on fine paper, sized and calendered, and bound in fancy cloth, flexible, with printed titles, etc., on sides and back; which, on account of the neat, convenient, and portable size of the volumes—particularly adapted for "railway reading"—we have styled "THE TRAVELLER'S EDITION." Seventeen volumes are now ready, embracing:

Pioneers.	Red Rover.	Sea Lions.
Mohicans.	The Water-Witch.	Wyandotte.
The Spy.	Wing-and-Wing.	Headsman.
The Prairie.	Two Admirals.	Wept of Wish-ton-Wish.
The Pathfinder.	The Pilot.	Lionel Lincoln.
The Deerslayer.	Bravo.	

Neat 16mo, uniformly bound in flexible covers, red cloth, per vol., . . $0 75

COOPER'S LEATHER STOCKING TALES, in Five Volumes, comprising:

Deerslayer.   Prairie.   Mohicans.   Pioneers.   Pathfinder.

Illustrated Edition, cloth, ... $7 50
People's Edition, cloth, uniform, gilt back and side, ... 5 00
"   "   extra sheep, library style, marble edges, . . . 6 00
"   "   half calf, or half turkey, ... 8 00
"   "   half calf, extra, full gilt backs, or antique, . . . 9 00

COOPER'S SEA TALES, Ten Volumes, comprising:

The Pilot.   Wing-and-Wing.   The Crater.
The Red Rover.   The Water-Witch.   Jack Tier.
The Two Admirals.   Afloat and Ashore.   The Sea Lions.
                      Miles Wallingford.

Illustrated Edition, cloth, ... $15 00
People's Edition, uniform cloth, gilt back and side, ... 10 00
"   "   sheep, extra, marble edges, library style, . . . 12 00
"   "   half calf, or half turkey, plain, ... 16 00
"   "   half calf, or half turkey, extra, full gilt backs, or antique, 18 00

NAVAL HISTORY OF THE UNITED STATES. By J. FENIMORE COOPER.

Abridged by himself, from the full work, for popular reading, with his latest corrections, and a continuance to 1856, from his unpublished MSS., and other authentic sources; including an account of the Japan Expedition; prepared by the Editor of the Octavo Edition. Illustrated with a fine Portrait of the Author on Steel, and Fifteen Illustrations of the principal Battle Scenes.

One vol., 12mo, gilt back and side, ... $1 25

DARLEY'S COOPER VIGNETTES.

A limited number of "Artist Proofs before letter" have been taken from each of the beautiful Steel Vignettes, engraved from Darley's Designs for the New Illustrated Edition of Cooper's Works. These are issued in folios, each containing eight proofs, and each proof accompanied with a page of letter-press descriptive of the picture, and embellished with a design on wood. The proofs are printed with the utmost care on India and backed on the finest French Plate Paper. Each folio is issued in a cover of highly ornamental design, printed in tint.

Complete in eight folios. Price per folio, ... $3 00

The Works of Charles Dickens.

HOUSEHOLD EDITION, Illustrated from Drawings by F. O. C. Darley and John Gilbert.

On March 1st, 1861, was commenced, in monthly issues, an entirely new edition of Dickens' Novels, from new stereotype plates, printed by Houghton, at the "Riverside Press," Cambridge, on superior *laid and tinted paper*, in style and form similar to Ticknor & Fields' popular Household Edition of the Waverley Novels. Great pains have been taken by the publishers to render this edition of Dickens' Works the most perfect series of books ever issued in America. The original drawings by Darley, whose designs for the Illustrated Edition of Cooper's Novels have been so distinguished, and the drawings by John Gilbert, the foremost of English draughtsmen, (this being the first time Mr. Gilbert has contributed original drawings to an American publication,) will give this edition a value possessed by no other, either English or American

This edition will have the author's latest prefaces and revisions, being reprinted from the last authorized London edition The entire series will be completed in fifty volumes. Each volume will contain an engraving on steel, in pure line and etching, from a drawing by Darley or Gilbert, the majority by Darley. Every issue will be a complete novel, and the publication will proceed as nearly as possible in the following order:

Pickwick,	4 vols.	Two Cities,	2 vols.
Oliver Twist,	2 "	Bleak House,	4 "
Nickleby,	4 "	Hard Times,	2 "
Curiosity Shop,	3 "	Little Dorrit,	4 "
Martin Chuzzlewit,	4 "	American Notes,	2 "
Barnaby Rudge,	3 "	Sketches,	2 "
Christmas Stories,	2 "	Uncommercial Traveller,	2 "
Dombey & Son,	4 "	Great Expectations,	2 "
Copperfield,	4 "		

STYLES AND PRICES.

Cloth, gilt back and side stamp,	per vol., · · · ·	$0 75
The same, uncut edges (English style), "	· · · ·	75
Half calf, extra, and antique,	" · · · ·	1 25

Any Novel may be had separate from the set.

A bound Prospectus, containing specimen pages and engravings, will be sent by mail, post-paid, to any person remitting 15 cents.

www.ingramcontent.com/pod-product-compliance
Lightning Source LLC
Chambersburg PA
CBHW020818030726
47496CB00009B/2936